1920

David B.
BLACK
PATHS

SELF
MADE
HERO

First published in English in 2011
by SelfMadeHero
5 Upper Wimpole Street
London W1G 6BP
www.selfmadehero.com

Written and Illustrated by: David B.
Colourist: Hubert
Translated from the French edition by Nora Mahony
c/o Parkbench Publishing Services

Editorial and Lettering: Lizzie Kaye
Publishing Director: Emma Hayley
With thanks to: Doug Wallace, Jane Laporte and Nick de Somogyi
David B. font provided by Coconino Press

First published in French by Futuropolis in 2008

A CIP record for this book is available from the British Library

ISBN: 978-1-906838-33-1

10 9 8 7 6 5 4 3 2

Printed and bound in China

1
Prologues

1919: in the wake of World War I, the defeated Austro-Hungarian Empire is losing control of the Adriatic port city of Fiume – to an eccentric group of idealist marauders, led by the Italian Fascist poet Gabriele d'Annunzio, a war hero turned self-styled "Pirate King". After storming the city with thousands of loyal foot soldiers, D'Annunzio declares Fiume a free Republic: a Utopian city-state immersed in the art and chaos of the avant-garde. Surrounded and besieged, the city descends into a bizarre, surrealist enclave of decadence, paranoia and impossible schemes.

D'Annunzio's grip on reality loosens, and the people of Fiume go hungry – among them the beautiful Mina, a smouldering cabaret singer haunted by an unhappy love affair, and Lauriano, tormented by the horror of the trenches, who searches in vain for the ghost of his comrade-in-arms who plagues his dreams.

For Claude Gendrot

...
Hey!
C'mon, it's open!
He took a hell of a beating, Paolo!
You know that guy outside?
We were in the same regiment!
He was in no fit state to recognize us anyway!

He had even less of a chance of recognizing us in our civvies.
Hmm...
I see!
?
What are your mates up to? It's unbelievable!
There are brawls like that every day!
We're bored stiff here!
Here we are! It's this door here.

I like that door!
You armed?
Course I'm armed. But I'll tell you what, no need for guns with the boys behind that door...
...Three punches in the gob, two kicks in the arse, and it'll be sorted!
There're four or five of 'em!
The door won't be hard to force.
Prologue: the bandits
You ready?

!
?
You ready?
...
Ah!
Nanini! What the hell are you doing here? What do you want?
We've come to get back the haul you stole from us!

Now that's it!
Go on!
Piss off!
OUT! GET OUT!
I told you, Natale, three swings, two kicks in the arse, and that'd be it done!
You see that? They were counting up our haul, those faggots.
This is all our stuff !
We're keeping the lot, that'll teach them!
ha ha ha ha ha ha
What are you doing here?

I'm Mina.
I guess I'm part of the haul.
You're the wife of one of the Milanese we just threw out?
Oh, no!
I was handsome Ferrara's girlfriend.
The Milanese chased him out of town yesterday so they could take over his trade.
I'm cold.
They took my clothes to prevent me from leaving.
They're in the room next door...
Would you have a cigarette?
Thank you.
These aren't the ones you're smoking!
Women don't like mine, the tobacco's too strong. I always have another case on me with lighter cigarettes.
Very smooth.
I'll go and find your clothes.
If you would.

What the hell were you up to?
There's a girl next door.
A girl?! Shit!
What the hell are you doing here?
Your friend was nicer!
HA!
You don't have to be nice to whores!
Get dressed, we're leaving.
Oh right! Where are you two going?
We have to leave now, the Milanese are going to come back with a crowd!
The Milanese are faggots! They won't come back. We're staying here. It's ours now!
Right! What do you think, Lauriano?
Me?
I think we can give the Milanese a second beating when they come back!
And I think that Lauriano is a very lovely name.

Hmm...
Shit! What the fuck are we going to do with this guy? He's not like us!
We're from the same regiment, him and me. We saved each other's lives many times during the war. I trust him!
He's a dirty bourgeois playing at gold-digging!
We're working, and he's having a laugh!
He'll leave us, I'm telling you!
He'll turn us over to the cops!
He will betray us!
Your colleague doesn't seem to like women much!
What's more, he doesn't like you either!
He's probably talking me down to Natale as we speak.
Doesn't that worry you?
Natale is my friend. We fought together. I know he'll stand up for me.
They've started fighting now.
Yes, they're fighting over me.

I was with a Sicilian grenadier – he saw me at the window and whistled at me.
There are some boys from my regiment, I should be with them!
Another soldier saw us (I was with him too), and they started fighting.
Then all their friends arrive and the Trojan War breaks out again...
So am I the beautiful Helen?
You are the new Helen, an electric Helen.
So shouldn't I get dressed then?

Hey!
Aren't you coming?
Mr. Dondina, Nerone is fighting with the others down there...
What the hell is that bloody idiot doing? Tell him to come here right now!
HEY!
NERONE!
WHAT? What is it?
Mr. Dondina's lookin' for you!
Nerone! Look at what you've done to your-self!
Why were you fighting? Over a woman?
Whooaa...
Noooooo!
I'm not such a fool I'd fight over a woman!

Well, that's something!
Natale Nanini, the "American", and the other young fella threw out our team and took our loot – we're going to make them dance.
The young fella?
His son?
You know him?
No, no one knows him. Always seems like he's there by chance, never says anything.
Nerone, you're already beaten up, you first!
The door's not strong, they've already forced it once...

Wouldn't dare come back, huh? Bright spark...
Isn't your friend Lauriano going to help us?
He's taking care of the girl...
WHAT?!
There's at least ten of them against only two of us!
Three punches and two kicks and it'll be sorted, that's what you said, right?
Pfff...
You're completely CRAZY!
... among other things.
See, from here we can reach that roof - there!
BAM!

The Milanese are here!
AH!
No time to waste...
?
?
COME ON, PUSH!

In a hurry, Natale?
How did I get myself into this?
You're an angel. You flew onto the roof...
You're joking!

Missed!
Ah!
They're there, on the roof!
Oh shit!
Get back from the window!

You OK, Natale?
Let's go...
It's Gianni!
Makes me sick to have killed one of them, but if it had to be, I'm glad it was him. I didn't like him.
You can see the whole square from here.
The fight looks like it's over...
Hey, Natale and Mike got out of it.
You can even see into the apartment we came from. Look, the Milanese are buzzing around like flies.

What do you think they're saying?
Every-thing they say is always so predictable!
You can see the whole city of Fiume from here!
Wow!
I like to come up here.
Prologue: the city
Down there, you can see the outposts of the Fiume "Arditi", and over there, the Italian army lines.
The First World War didn't stop on 11 November 1918...
...it scattered.

In Eastern Europe, old countries are reborn, and new ones appear.
Romania
Armenia
Estonia
Borders twist like poisonous snakes.
Hungary
1
9
Turkey
Poland
These young countries turn on each other to cut their teeth.
Latvia
Ukraine
1
When they run out of enemies, they massacre the Jews.
8
Lithuania
In the Orient, they decimate Christian communities.

1919
The British General Wavell, who had participated in discussions about the Treaty of Versailles, summed it up...
"After the 'War to end War' they seem to have been pretty successful at making a 'Peace to end Peace'."
A journalist interviewing an anonymous member of a Franco-German corps who was fighting in the improbable Baltic wars got a simpler answer...
The war is over, the peace treaty is signed - why do you continue to fight?
Who decided that the war was over?
We are the war!
The victors came to Versailles for their spoils.

Italy got a certain number of territories, but they were refused Dalmatia and the port of Fiume, which the Allies gave to Yugoslavia.

FIUME IS OURS!

The inhabitants of Fiume, mostly Italians, were demanding to be brought back under Italian control.

There were also people whom the government had sent to war who liked it there, and wanted to continue fighting for their own cause.

They found a leader - a poet and a soldier. His name was Gabriele D'Annunzio.

Before the war his works had been known all over Europe. He fought for Italy to enter the war on the side of the Allies.

He signed up when he was over fifty, served in the navy and the air force, and lost an eye in combat.

Commandant D'Annunzio arrived in Fiume on 12 September leading a troop made up of ex-Arditi, deserters and soldiers who had rallied to his cause.
He offered the city to the Italian government, which, under pressure from the Allies, surrounded them and ordered D'Annunzio to surrender.
He refused, and proclaimed Fiume an independent republic.
The only people to recognize this new state were the members of the Berlin Dada Club.
Fiume was included in the Dada Almanac.

1920
Six months later...
The Italian army is still surrounding the city...
...but there aren't any battles.
The Italian government hopes that the situation will deteriorate and that the city will fall by itself...
...that way, there won't be any bloodshed.
From here you can see the windows of the government building. That's where D'Annunzio works.
...no liberation front can leave from anywhere but Fiume.

There, we'll send that to all the revolutionary groups in the world.
I'll make copies.
Don't forget to send one to the Holy See.
What should we call our "Anti-Society of Nations"?
A name... yes... We must find a name that will resonate around the world.
Names are very important. Naming is power!
Commandant, Mr Harukichi Shimoï is here, he brings a message from Benito Mussolini.
Let him in!
Let him in, this son of the Rising Sun.
Let him beam his rays upon us, the eternal youth of ancient Asia!

I'm coming...
Mussolini is putting his Fascists at my disposal and has proposed that I march on Rome!
I have a call from the Subcarpathian Ruthenia Liberation Army.
Let's gather all the revolutionary forces and take Rome!
Are the Fascists revolutionaries?
Has anyone seen my town planning dossier?
Prologue: the poet
We're going to raze the city to the ground.
The Fascists reject the old order, so they're revolutionaries!
We will build a modern city, which will be called FUTURISTA!
...the Ruthenian people and those of Fiume are brothers, there is no doubt...
...but we can't MARCH on Rome, we need to go as fast as possible, in an armoured train!
I saw Chicherine in Zurich; an entente with the Soviets is possible...
The Masonic lodges of Central Europe are with us!
We have to attack Rome by air!
We have to recognize the USSR!
I wrote to the directors of the Italian asylums to ask them to send all the madmen to Fiume!

Madmen have wonderful ideas; we can take them as advisors!
We should make our soldiers do yoga.
...and the Triads!
We must use the pirate republics as a model!
We must restore the Roman Empire!
We must raise the alarm worldwide!
We'll have women fight for freedom alongside men!
Campanella dreamed of "The City of Sun"; we'll make Fiume the city of life!
Commandant, there's someone to see you.
sterile institutions dried-up laws!
I'm busy! I'm not here - for anyone!
Fiume will be the avant-garde of life!
It's just that... he insists, Commandant. His name is Crispi, but he says his surname is "Maciste".
MACISTE! Let him in right away!
Do you know him, Commandant?
Not at all...
...but Gabriele D'Annunzio can't not receive a man by the name of "Maciste"!
Comman-dant, I am Comm-issioner Crispi.
Masonic hand-shake.

May we speak somewhere quieter?
Come in here, brother, and it'll give you some hope.
Oh!
It's your famous collection of objets d'art.
Only part of it...
That's what I wanted to talk to you about.
Can I offer you a drink?

Never in the morning.
You see this statue? It was stolen from the Baptistry of San Girolamo...
It's a superb Saint Francis from the end of the 14th century.
The pair of revolvers isn't part of the original, I put them there.
I am the Milanese Commissioner of Police. I'm investigating trafficked stolen goods, and all my leads are pointing to Fiume.
There are gangs pillaging the city and moving their stolen goods to Milan, Rome and to France.
As you've declared Fiume a free territory, I can't investigate here.
I would like a laissez-passer document, signed by you. It's in our interest that these gangs that are profiting from the chaos...
HA!
What chaos?
Don't confuse chaos with freedom, Mr. Maciste!

So...
We have our laissez-passer, my dear Commish!
Bravo!
So there are quite a few people waiting...
There's all sorts!
Balkan conspirators, idiots savants, artistes maudits, double, triple and quadruple agents, utopians, party men...
It's the city of dreams - all the dreamers have come to sleep here.
And there you are, right in front of everyone!
Ha! I'm "Maciste"!
That's what the Milanese gangs nicknamed me.

Commandant D'Annunzio is an extraordinary man. He's a poet, a playwright... He's even written for the cinema.
He created the character of Maciste for the film Cabiria. You didn't see it?
Uhhhh, no.
I knew he'd let me in with Maciste as my "open sesame"...
...and because I'm a Freemason.
He offered me champagne in a skull.
NO!
In a skull?! Whoooo.
Yeah...
He's an extraordinary man. If I were younger, I'd be right here with him!
Oh and one more thing - they say he sleeps on a pillow stuffed with his mistresses' hair!
Whoa, now that I like!
Nowadays, women have short hair, and we're far too old.
Investigating is our only pleasure now.

Come, now, not our only one. I know a girl in a little brothel on via della Mosca in Milan, who's something else...
Mmm...
Will you take me?
I promise!
I'm French...
I already saw you on the posters.
Really?
Well, you're eagle-eyed! Did you recognize me right away in that bedroom?
Of course.

Ahhh, so that's why you kissed me...
But - it was you who kissed me!
Cheeky! It was you!
I took you in my arms to reassure you, and you kissed me.
You did!
How did you end up in that bedroom - and in Fiume?
I came here so that you'd kiss me!
Ha ha ha...
Mmm...
Prologue: the lovers
How did I get here?
I met Ferrara when I was heartbroken, and he brought me here.

He used to say that here you could only love the girl who had come to sing you love songs!
Ferrara got to trafficking all sorts of things right away.
I kept singing, life was beautiful...
I never saw you at the cabaret.
I'm eagle-eyed too.
I saw you, but you couldn't have seen me. I was in the wings.
We were talking business with Ferrara and Natale who you saw just now.
You have to look in dark corners to see you...

I prefer the shadows.
Why do you hide?
What are you hiding from?
I'm not hiding, I'm just not part of the crowd anymore, that's all.
What did you do in the war?
I was in the Arditi, in the assault troops. I look like a civilian now, but I'm still a soldier.
I've heard about the Arditi. They were awful.
Yes! We fought like dogs.
Shit!
Oh, sorry...
Don't be, it's the right word for it.

It's a smell I remember very well.
I remember stabbing a guy in the stomach, and he shat his trousers.
Not very romantic. Tell me about the love affair you were talking about.
It was a great passion. It flared up, and then...
Do you know that song? I'll sing it, just for you...
?
They got together one summer, then all of a sudden they argued and foolishly parted.
Meanwhile, good married folk are cuckolded and happy.
Love doesn't care about lovers!*
*Gaston Couté

Is that a warning?
It applies to both of us...
Were you hurt by how things turned out?
Yes...
?
It's another fight. Let's get out of here...
?
Hey there, you saw something... Was it a girl or someone suspicious?
A suspicious girl...

I met her in France during the war. She's Romanian or Hungarian, I can't remember which... She worked with her father for the German secret services.
She changed sides for love, for a French agent.
That's a nice story.
I don't trust nice stories with rogue heroines.
What are we going to do?
Are the Milanese going to want vengeance?
For now, we can't risk anything.
They're going to put their haul somewhere safe and hide their dead, which will take a bit of time.
Where are we going?

I'm staying in an attic with some officers from my regiment.
But I also took a little room for some peace and quiet. I can take you there if you'd like.
CORA
Yes, I really would.
I can't risk being seen!
ERVI
I can't sing at the Palazzo any more.
And singing is my life.

The Milanese won't take it out on you, just on Natale and me...
In any case, you have to show them that you sing!
We're here. That woman is the land-lady.
Mrs. Rivabella, I wanted to speak to you.
I met Miss Mina here in Fiume. She's an old friend, and I wanted to know if...
Oh my good man, I'm just off to Mass! Let's chat after, if it's all the same to you...
What luck, I was just saying I must go to church... after I've had a quick peek at the room.

I have nowhere to stay, and we wanted to ask you if I might live here...
Ah...
Well...
I'll go up and look and I'll come right back down.
Ummm... yes... then I'll wait for you here.
"I was just saying I must go to church" - that's rich!
You're mean. You're going to up and leave me...
You're going to go and see your friend Natale and I'm going to be all alone.
And I don't like being all alone...
I'll come back tonight.
When you're at the cabaret, make sure there's always someone with you.

You write?
A bit... I'm secretary to Guido Keller, who's secretary to D'Annunzio!
He publishes this magazine. It's called Yoga. I write articles for it every now and then.
„YOGA"
Can you write songs for me?
Hmm...
That's something I've never done... I'll try.
Now kiss me. I don't think Mrs. Rivabella would want to see that!
She should!

Well, Crispi?
Masonic hand-shake.
Commissioner Brass, security.
Prologue: the investigators
We've got it, Captain Ruffolo! The Commandant gave me a laissez-passer!
I was so sure that you'd get it, I started researching without waiting for it!
Now!
What's he doing there?
The soldiers brought it here for you from a government building, along with a letter...
To the valiant Commissioner Maciste. This statue belongs to italy, and i am returning it to her. Accept the pair of revolvers as a homage to poetry and justice.
"Commandant D'Annunzio".

So, how do I look?
They looked better on the statue.
?
There's a mirror here, if you'd like to look.
Ha ha ha...
I look like such an arsehole, I almost want to keep them.
Enough!
Ruffolo, have them sent back to the commandant on behalf of an official to an engineer.
What about the case?
There was a confrontation between two gangs in a building on Piazza dei Caduti.
Here we have a Milanese gang who are causing some damage!
Ah, those are mine!
The Milanese and another gang were fighting over a stash holed up in that apartment. They half killed each other!
Any witnesses?
The neighbours. It's a bit messy because there was a huge brawl in the square at the same time.

Some of them said they'd seen a man and a woman escape over the rooftops.
But before escaping, the man shot into the apartment.
Did you send someone up there?
He shot from the roof?
He shot from the roof!
I sent Amedeo, one of my carabinieri. He found a casing from a Colt 45.
A 45?
That's a pretty rare calibre in Europe...
Our American allies have been bringing Colt 45s in since they arrived in 1917.
American or not, our shooter must have been a soldier... or an ex-soldier. And we're hardly short of them here!
If we ever found him, his arrest would be a delicate matter - they're very loyal to each other.
They make the laws!
And we'll have to see what kind!
CARABIN

I came to Fiume with my carabinieri because I wanted to support Commandant D'Annunzio.
He described everything we were dreaming of after this war in such beautiful language, he enchanted us.
Disappointed?
I wasn't expecting such chaos!
I must say, it's one hell of a mess.
Sometimes it's a beautiful mess...
But some mornings, after a frantic night of fighting between drunken or drugged soldiers, what emerges from the mayhem is a sadness and stupidity that disgusts me!
It's hard enough to survive in a city with a poet for its president. We can't speak in verse all the time!
And anyway, despite having deserted the Italian army to serve an illegitimate regime, I still have some sense of duty - or at least of the importance of some kind of balance.
If I could be cynical for a moment, we can profit from this mess.
How so?
If there aren't any laws there's no need to respect them.

You think I waited for you?!
I'm going to give you a tour of the city...
We're going to see some Colt 45s!
Here, everyone walks around armed to the teeth like a Balkan revolutionary.
These days, we do what we can...
Which is to say that we do great things!
Come, come...
See that, Crispi? That's the girl I was telling you about earlier.

I'd like to have a few words with her...
Lord...
Lord, please let me get out of this town.
I beseech you, please let me be a famous singer, too.
The most famous in the whole world...
Lord, hear our prayer!

There he is!
There's going to be a parade!
Will there be food too?
Prologue: the end
YESTERDAY THERE WAS NO WHEAT LEFT IN FIUME! TODAY...
OUR BREAD BASKETS ARE FULL!
Our pirates have brought a boat into
So strong!
What a voice!
Mr. Dondina, we have started to move our haul out of town.
port that is full of
Good, good!

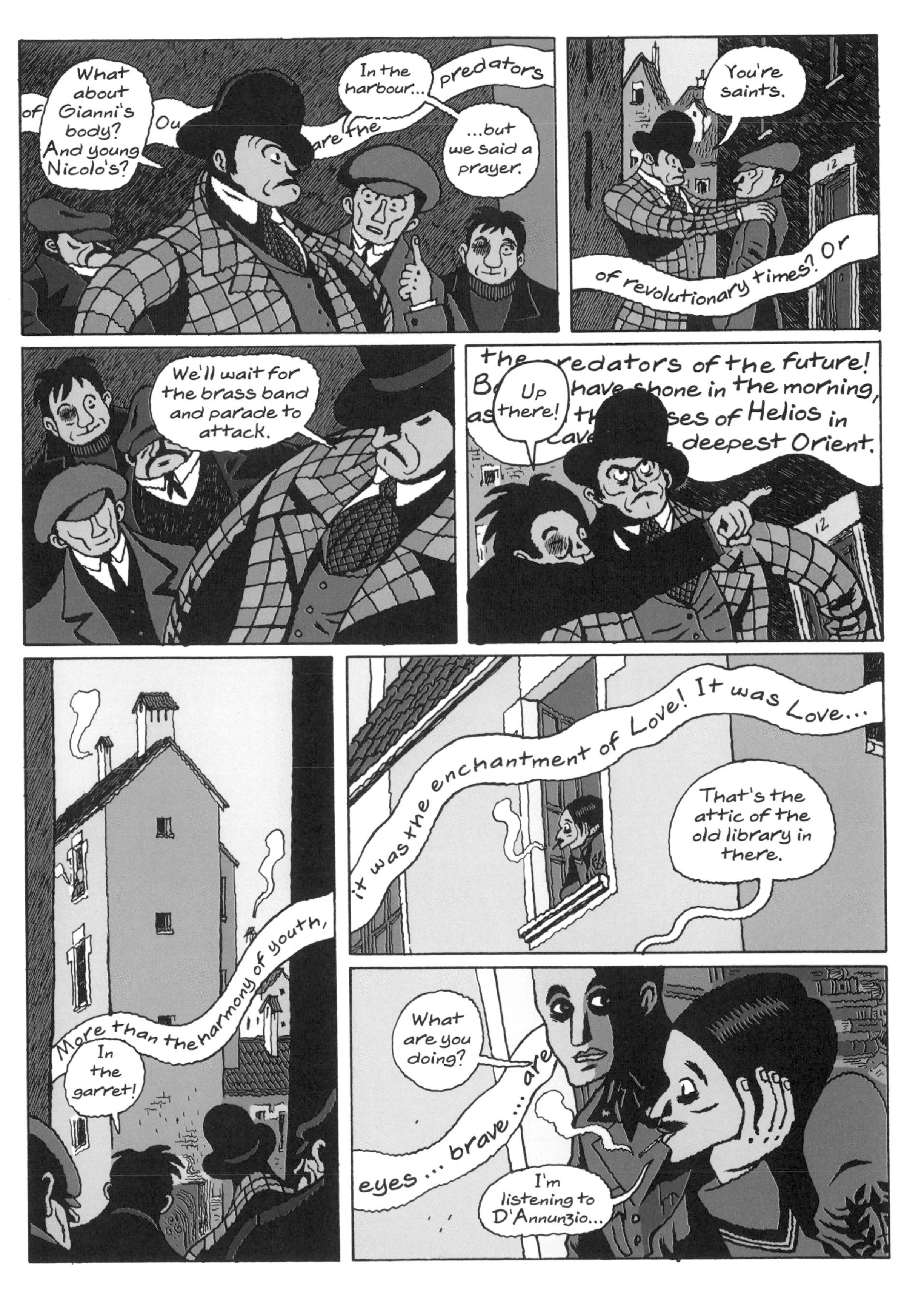
What about Gianni's body? And young Nicolo's?
of
Ou
are the
In the harbour...
predators
...but we said a prayer.
You're saints.
of revolutionary times? Or
We'll wait for the brass band and parade to attack.
the predators of the future!
have shone in the morning,
ses of Helios in
deepest Orient.
Up there!
More than the harmony of youth,
In the garret!
it was the enchantment of Love! It was Love...
That's the attic of the old library in there.
What are you doing?
eyes ... brave ... are
I'm listening to D'Annunzio...

Italian ... men ... if not ... starving ... and the...
We can't hear him from here.
and the...
I don't care what he's saying! It's the rhythm of his speech that I like.
There were four of them who had fought together in the same unit of the Arditi.
Da da da da... it's a march! It's our march!
A march in a town that's surrounded. We'd end up marching in a circle.
You're right, Cesare, we're suffocating here...
Worse stilll....
We're bored stiff.
They had moved into the attic of the old library because so many soldiers had arrived.
I'll kill myself!
Again?
Tomorrow I'll be back on my feet and out of here!
Are you and Lauriano still up to your old bullshit?

Cesare and Lauriano loved books, and enjoyed surrounding themselves with them..
I fought hard, risked my neck, lived like a dog in the stinking trenches...
And now my life is all cigars and silk shirts!
Natale, we were brothers in arms. You know that I love you, but all the wonderful energy you have could be put to better use!
Bahhhh... I see you with your politics, but I want it all, and I want what's coming to me now.
Natale and Gaetano made night stands, stools and shelves out of the books.
We want everything right away, too. We have a piece of that in Fiume - now, we have to go and get the rest in Rome.
they stayed hidden for many days
they fed themselves with... thoughts... and happiness...
It's good, his speech, huh?
It's good, but it's long!
Lauriano, don't you have anything to say?
horse
No, you never have anything to say. You've already left.

They had instinctively constructed a sort of trench from the piles and piles of books.
Guido Keller's looking for you all over.
He wants to know if you've written your article for Yoga magazine.
I have an idea...
It will be something on the "Land of No-Where". You know, the legendary country in Iranian mythology.
No-Where?
That's you all over, that is. It'll be an autobiography, then?
You could see it like that...
That's the band - the parade's starting! Come on!
Nerone, break down the door!
Now that I'm dumb enough to do!
And you're wasting your talent and precious time writing this nonsense.
l' Incrocio di Ecate
It was you who wrote this, wasn't it?
INCIDENTS de la NU
Dragone
Prezzo: 5 lire

No, it wasn't me.
You're lying, Lauriano!
ZIOI
You'd rather write pulp serials than write for Yoga.
Lunedi
n°
la NUIT
But I'm telling you, it wasn't me...

BOOOM
They must be all mincemeat in there!
Shit! Shit! Shit!

BROTHERS, ATTACK!
Gaetano, don't be stupid!
GAETANO!
BIBL
Coming through.
'Scuse me.
'Scuse me.
Move it! GO!
BIB
Hey, you...

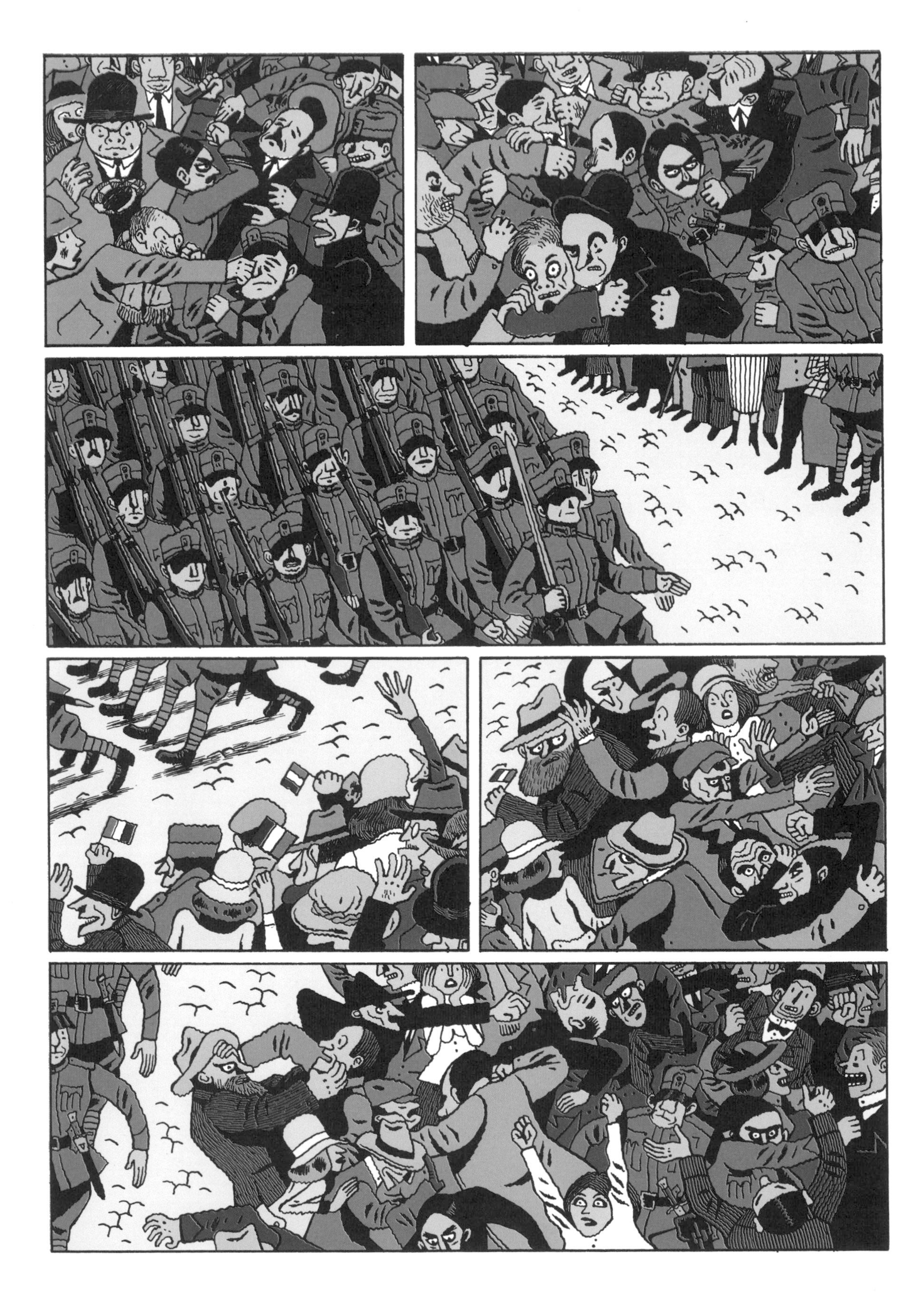

What people! What energy! What virility!
I'm proud to lead people made of such stern stuff!
Hmm...
Where were we...?
I was saying...
We have to pick a date for the worldwide revolution.
So...
I've got something on the 18th, but we could do it the next day.
The riot continued all day.
It rolled through the town like an angry sea.

In the darkness, it descended into fisticuffs.
Dusk - and the lights of home...
home...
PALAZZO
Smile through the rain...
And let us fill with love and song...
The lamplit hour.
PALAZZO
La la la

They're still fighting down there...
What are you doing, Lauriano?
?
I'm doing my cat-burglar routine.
I'm going to look for Gaetano, and maybe fight a bit myself...
Very well, I'll see if the Milanese come back this way...
I'm not sure this is exactly what I want.
But I don't have much choice...

2
The Ghosts

Well...
I made love to her.
That was too fast.
I would have liked to have got there slowly.
I would have liked to have taken my time...
In Fiume, you can find anything but time...
Paper, my good sir?
A paper?
Why not?
Doesn't matter which...
Thank you, sir.

?
But...
Ohh...
Hey!
Grandad!
You don't like the news?
I have others...
It's not that, it's that this paper is dated 1912!
I thought you were selling today's paper!
Look at this...
1910, 1910, 1911. This one's 1902...
I only sell papers from the old days...
Because in those ones...
...there's no war!
Hah!

That's a fantastic reason.
It's the only one worth having!
I'd like to know one thing.
Would you, by any chance, describe yourself as a happy man?
I lost my legs twenty years ago, so happiness catches up with me often enough.
Riddle me that...
...
Alright, Lauriano?
Musing on the passing of the years, are you?
Gaetano?
We didn't see you fighting all night.
I was with a girl.
I was the one who sparked off the riot last night.

You're more than capable of that!
This morning I was the last one standing!
Have a look at the war wounds.
Whooo...
Superb!
You've earned two medals to hang your glasses on!
Don't poke fun, I'm suffering here!
You're suffering, but enough of your black eyes!
So, bruiser, you got out alive!
Natale! You're up and about?
I'd had enough of staying in bed because of a little slip of the knife - it was nothing.
A propos, I just saw your Milanese friend go by.
Ah.
Cesare...
The one who walks along squirming like this.
Hey, Cesare...
Dondina?
I don't have a name for guys like that, I just know that he's after you - so I'm warning you.

He had the same idea as you!
He's in uniform too!
Your shoot-out from yesterday is in the paper.
You hear that, Lauriano? We're stars.
Cesare, drop the exasperated attitude and spit it out!
You already know my concerns. Italy needs militants, they already have enough bandits.
I am a militant!
I'm an anarchist!
All the bandits say that, and there's no one more bourgeois than them.
Cocaine, Cesare?
I practised magic and yoga all night long. They're much more effective than drugs.
Anyone else?

No way.
It was good for keeping your edge in the trenches, but we don't need it any more.
Here, we'll get coffees instead.
Mario! Four!
Mine's a double.
Snap!
I have a meeting with Shimoï, Mussolini's envoy.
It's about time we became warriors again.
You should come with me, my friends.
You have to salute all the time with the Fascists. I'm tired just thinking about it.
Go on, go on, you'll tell us.
Oh!
?
?
?

GRAN CAFE ITALIA
Did he see a girl?
Or was it a ghost?
With Lauriano, it could well be either.
Or he's afraid that you'll take him to the Fascists.
That's another possibility.
Leone...
Leone?
Is that you?
Leone! Wait for me...

Leone!
?
Leone, don't go.
Leone.

Mr. Dondina...
There.
Look, it's Natale Nanini's friend!
Him over there, with the blue coat.
What're you waiting for? Get him for yesterday!
Leave him alone, poor bugger.
Absolutely no noise - do it with a knife!

Leone, it was you.
You came to see me.
You wanted to tell me some-thing.
Why did you disappear so soon?
AH!
♪
One down!
Don't turn around!
Sir?
Is he ill?
Did he trip?
He's drunk!
I was hit!

The old man's paper!
The journal with no war...
It saved my life.
It's just an old, torn-up paper!
That it is...
Leone...
You came to warn me that they wanted to kill me.
Huh?
Is that it?
It was a sign.
But I don't believe in signs.
I never have.

I don't believe in ghosts.
And you know that full well - we talked about it often.
So why did you appear to me?
I was out for the count!
Lauriano took his chance to sneak out.
No doubt he's up on the roof doing his cat routine.
I'd rather...
...have woken up between his paws!
He's always on the go.

Books, papers, magazines...
Nick Carter, Fantômas, Ghost Ranger.
Incidents de la Nui.
Yoga.
Ultra.
It's a portrait of Lauriano in newsprint.
It's such a boy's room, there's not even a mirror.
I must look as bad as him.
Ah, Mr. Uniform. Something tells me Lauriano won't wear you again.

I'll go.
I have to go take a bath at Mrs. Riva-bella's.
And I'll try to find the flesh-and-blood Lauriano!
Here's my plan for the Futurist armoured train.
I'll need another one to carry my collections!
So, it's decided. We'll attack Yugoslavia!?
I'll take this car here for my headquarters!
Locomo

SF
Our Croatian and Slovenian brothers stand by us in this action.
They will revolt against the power of Belgrade once our troops cross the border.
We'll win over the Italian troops that surround us!
All you'll have to do is go to the outposts.
Benito Mussolini and the Fascists will support you in your efforts.
How will this support manifest itself? Money?
I'll go mounted on a white horse.
Guido! Guido Keller!
Look, it's my armoured train. We're going to reconquer Dalmatia!

Armoured cars with racing engines will patrol alongside the train to protect it!
It will be a Futurist war!
The world war was faster and faster!
We must be faster!
Yes! Speed, speed!
What've you got there, Guido?
The first issue of our paper.
"Yoga. The magazine for Free Spirits."
,,YOGA"
Why didn't you submit the articles to me before printing them?
?
I could have given advice.
Helped.
Inspired.
,,YOGA"
This blank page is idiocy, Guido!

A friend didn't finish his article in time!
I held out in the hope that it would turn up, one way or another!
WHERE
Did you come with someone?
Him?
He's a madman.
I wrote to the directors of mental asylums asking them to send me their most delirious residents.
Madmen have magnificent ideas, pure genius – they are completely untouched by the barbs of conscience.
I would have liked your paper to serve my policy rather than create Dadaism.
This is a critical moment!
You're the one who's critical – a poet, spouting such clichés!

All moments are critical – every single minute is critical.
Spending them with joy is what counts.
NO WHERE
These are the most beautiful and profound pages in the whole magazine!
They're as deep as the trenches, and good luck to anyone trying to understand them!
YOGA
Conquering Dalmatia by train is bourgeois!
Ha...
There are many more battles still to fight here in Fiume!
Don't confuse your enemies, Gabriele. We're fighting them!
Watch out, Guido. Don't go too far, or else...
Or else you and your Fascist friends will set fire to Yoga's offices, just like you did to Avanti's?!*
*The Milan offices of the socialist newspaper were destroyed by the Fascists on 15 April 1919.

Come, come, gentlemen! We're all on the same side, despite appearances!
Do you think that Mussolini is going to send you his troops?
Don't you realize that you've become competition to him?
While he's pushing you into unlikely adventures, he's busy taking over power in Italy!
He's sending you his Japanese emissary to promise the world to you!
Guido, that's unfair!
Mr. Shimoï brought money that Mussolini collected from all over Italy to finance the revolution in Fiume!
That's marvellous!
And how much did Il Duce take from the total amount?
I'm begging you to deny it, Mr. Shimoï!
Hmm...
So? Answer him. What did he take? Half?
...A bit more, I think...

It's not possible...
Tell Mussolini that people are dying of hunger in Fiume, that we don't have enough coal to keep warm!
...
That we're living off of looted ships!
Mussolini is using that money to finance the Fascist Party. He's going to do great things!
What about me? Should I cook up some macaroni?
You little fanatical toy soldier, you're the one who's stirring things up!
Stop!

STOP IT
RIGHT NOW!
Bloody hell!
PAM
PAM
Don't make me shoot into the crowd!
Everything alright, Commandant?
I was just finishing a poem...

Right!
Let's finish the long poem of our friendship right here!
As far as wearing a uniform goes, I'm not wearing anything but the uniform of my very own army!
My skin.
Oh, no no no. Don't you get undressed.
Guido! Come back! Where are you going?
I'm taking my aeroplane, Gabriele, and I'm going back to Russia to lead the turncoat army.
Or I could fly over the Vatican and drop roses in homage to Saint Francis of Assisi.
Guido, you're right, but I'm too old to follow you.

Too old to go naked.
Too old to pilot a plane with only one eye.
Offer a rose to Saint Francis for me.
I will.
Goodbye.
Would someone have some cocaine?
Lauriano!
Guido!
At least you're not in uniform!
Why are you naked?
I gave everything to Gabriele D'Annunzio! I'm free!

Did you show him Yoga?
He didn't like it!
He wanted to oversee the magazine. He started taking himself very seriously all of a sudden, and he had a whole gang of reactionaries around him.
When I came to Fiume, he said to me, "To command well is to relinquish command."
I don't want to command or be commanded!
It's November. Please, take my coat.
Guido, I saw Leone...
Leone died at the Piave!
It was his ghost, of course.
Of course!
I often see the dead - people I know, or not, whole or in pieces.
I have to bury Leone somehow.

We can organize a symbolic burial for our dead comrades who have no graves!
The dead are naked too!
We must appease the souls who wander among us.
Not a burial - a wake!
Do you know her?
Who?
The girl standing behind you!

Hello, I'm looking for Lauriano.
You're the girl from yesterday, the one he snuck out with over the roof-tops.
Sneaking out over rooftops earns you a seat.
Are you friends of Lauriano's?
We're each a particular kind of friend.
Natale is his friend from the slums.
And he and I studied together.
Whoo... me and studies...
I saw all his books, his papers, all the things he writes.
He took you to his room? To his Land of No-Where?
Yes, but I never heard him talk about this land.

It's a country with a heap of names: the Seventh Climate, the Seventy-two Universe, the Green Isle, the Second World, the Interworld, the Other Side of the Mountain, Lower Malakut, the Three Cities, the Country of the Invisibles, the Emerald Country...
It means that Cesare... well, he's a complicated thing, Oriental, complicated, like carpets or Turkish Delight.
Lauriano believes in this No-Where without believing in it, but still believing in it a little.... that's what he's like.
Something happened to Lauriano.
Ah.
In 1918 he was at the front at the Piave.
We were all in the Arditi assault troops.
Gaetano was there too, he had just arrived, and Leone, a really young guy, and Pipò and Andrea and...
They ordered us to launch an assault by day.
We had received new supplies.

It was summertime. They made us attack as soon as the enemy started their evening meal.
The armour protected us and slowed us down.
TJ1

In our armour we became a pack of steel dogs.
RETREAT!
LAURIANO! COME BACK!

Don't lag behind, Lauriano...
Night is falling...
Don't give me orders, help me take off this armour!
We have to hurry, the artillery fire will start soon.
I can run faster than you!
Where's Leone?
He's up ahead with the prisoners.
Leone!

Leone was the fifth member of the gang.
He was like our little brother.
We hit a net of barbed wire.
That's when the shells started to fall.
Natale and I managed to get behind friendly lines.
What about Lauriano?
Lauriano wasn't among the survivors.
The cease-fire came at about midnight.
We were sure that he was hiding in a shell-hole and that he'd come and find us...
And that Leone was with him.
The front was calm during the days that followed.
One night, we slid into no-man's-land.

We found him stretched out in a crater. It looked like he was waiting for us.
I came back, I wanted to see you again.
But... you didn't come back. We came to find you.
He had this look about him... and we took him back.
Oh, I know that look all too well.
He told us what had happened to him.
He hid in a hole to escape the bombing.

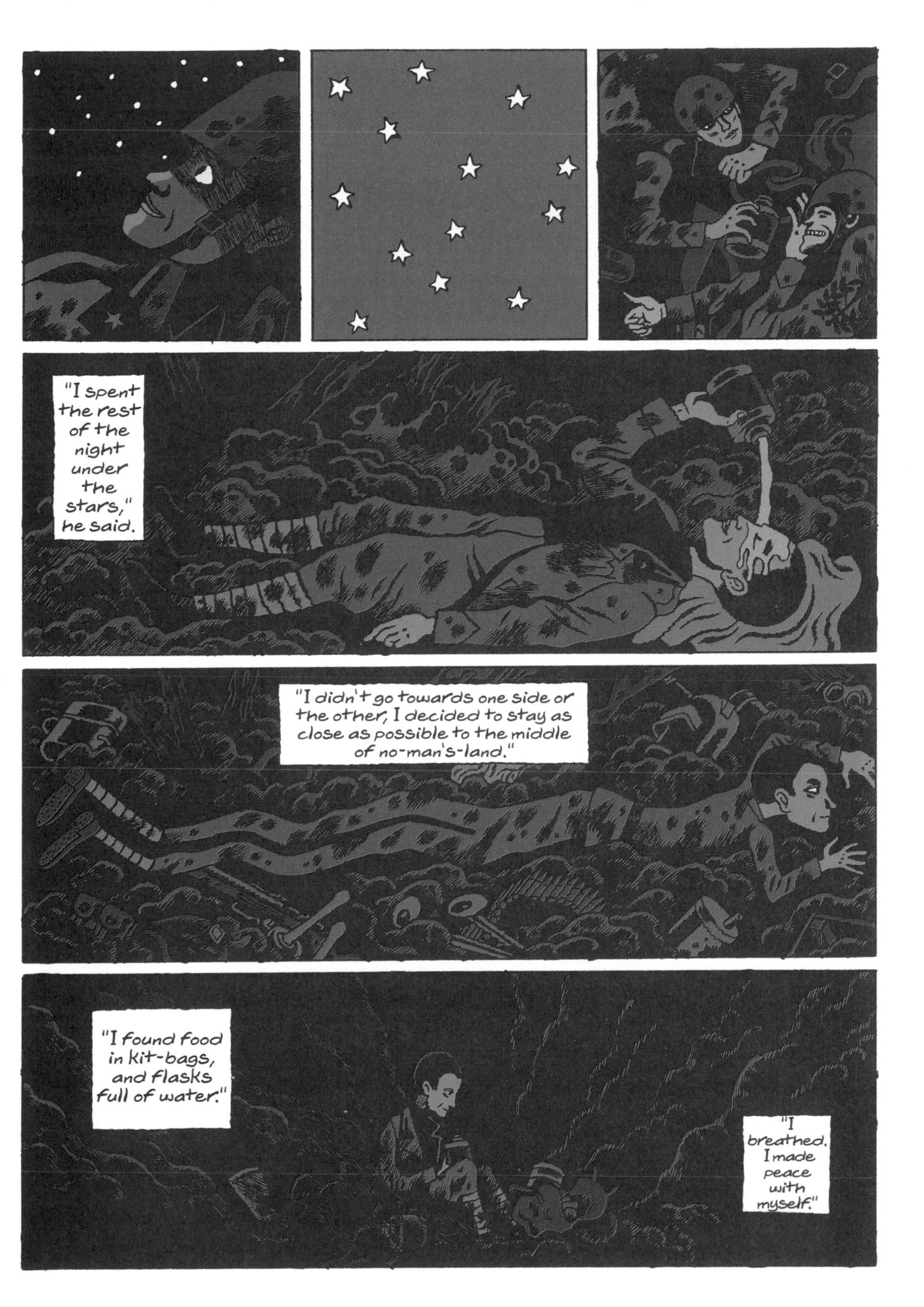
"I spent the rest of the night under the stars," he said.
"I didn't go towards one side or the other, I decided to stay as close as possible to the middle of no-man's-land."
"I found food in kit-bags, and flasks full of water."
"I breathed. I made peace with myself."

"The animals came to pay tribute."
"Then the ghosts appeared."
34
12
"Leone was among them."
I would like you to bury me.
But my body went up in smoke in the shell explosion.
How can I give you a burial if you don't have a body any more?
It's an impossible task, but you must do it all the same.

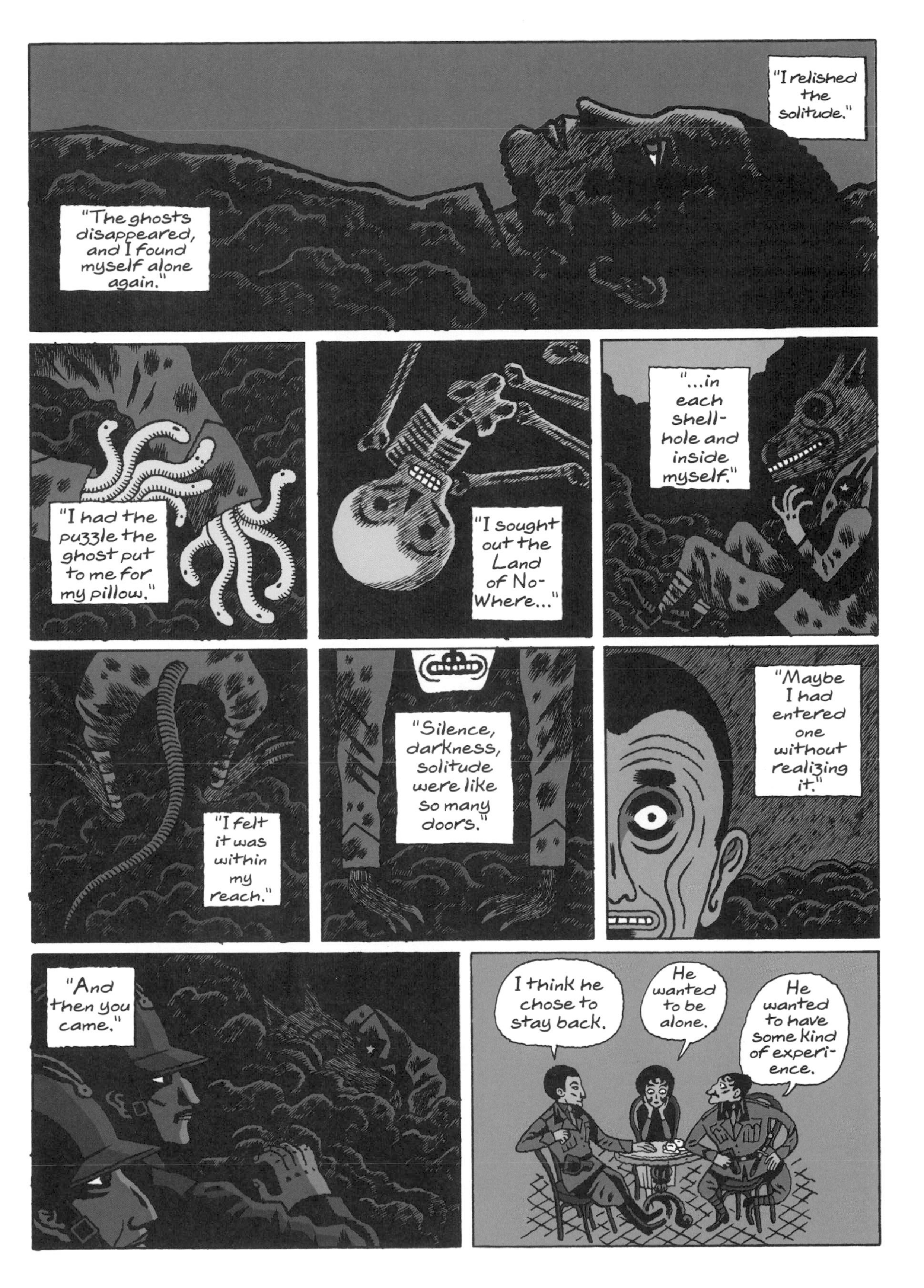
"I relished the solitude."
"The ghosts disappeared, and I found myself alone again."
"I had the puzzle the ghost put to me for my pillow."
"I sought out the Land of No-Where..."
"...in each shell-hole and inside myself."
"I felt it was within my reach."
"Silence, darkness, solitude were like so many doors."
"Maybe I had entered one without realizing it."
"And then you came."
I think he chose to stay back.
He wanted to be alone.
He wanted to have some kind of experi-ence.

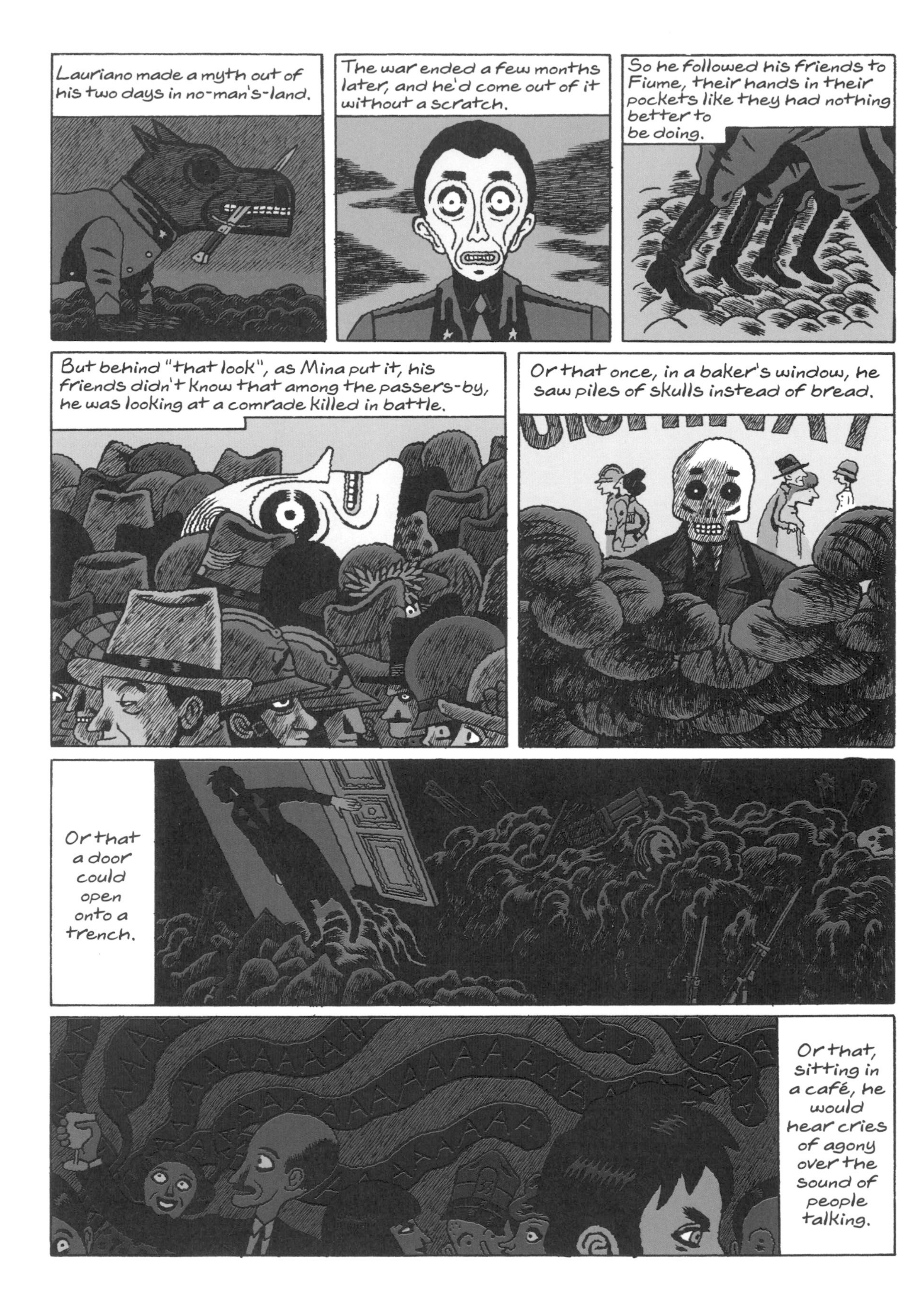
Lauriano made a myth out of his two days in no-man's-land.
The war ended a few months later, and he'd come out of it without a scratch.
So he followed his friends to Fiume, their hands in their pockets like they had nothing better to be doing.
But behind "that look", as Mina put it, his friends didn't know that among the passers-by, he was looking at a comrade killed in battle.
Or that once, in a baker's window, he saw piles of skulls instead of bread.
Or that a door could open onto a trench.
Or that, sitting in a café, he would hear cries of agony over the sound of people talking.

To him, rubbish piled up in the street took on the shape of a mound of dead bodies.
Look!
We're going to end up like them...
Ha! Life is good in the "Free City of Fiume"!
We're going to die of cold and hunger.
Hmm...
Don't touch things with your shoes, you can see that you're making them dirty!
My shoes are cleaner than your rags.
Hey, soldier!
You looking for a new uniform?

I was just saying...
Hey!
Arditi! Come attack my trench!
Sorry, I'm not on duty!
Natale, I have a plan!
A plan that involves heat and food?
You want to steal D'Annunzio's collection?
Sing it louder and we can all dance to it!
I heard every-thing!
EVERY-THING!
DOMANI
Ha ha ha, you should see your faces!
Lauriano, you're not funny.
Not funny at all!
I never thought you were funny either, Bertoni.

You're a plain old gangster, a bandit!
Pfff...
Ha...
You want to steal D'Annunzio's collection? You're right - like you, it's worthless!
It's nothing but trinkets! There is something that's very valuable, though...
It's not in the collection any more...
...but I know where to find it.
And I'm going to steal that. Natale - you're welcome to come for the heist.
So you were spying on us?
No, I was down the back with Guido!
I saw you arrive and I came to play a joke on you.
We're planning a cele-bration.
A celebration of the dead who died without a proper burial.

You mean Leone?
Yes.
I still see him sometimes.
Yes. That's good, we should do something for our dead. I'll go to that party.
Pfff...
What would you know? As soon as the war started, you snuck off to America!
"Mike" Bertoni! Pfff...
Come on, tell me all about what we're stealing - and how.
What's with the paper? Are you hiding?
No, I'm dead!
It's my new face...
Natale, we're going to steal a statue of Saint Francis!
It's in the carabinieri's barracks...
Lauriano, you're mad!
...in the captain's office.

My friends, I've just received my cases.
It's the sign that our beautiful free city of Fiume is in its final days.
?
At each of my new postings, I've waited for my luggage. It always arrives just as I'm transferred elsewhere.
Any news about the Milanese?
Have a look out the window.
Dondina's going by...
We could get them from here!
I'll go you one better, and funnier.
Have a look at what they're passing out in the street.
A masked ball.
A danse macabre.
A cele-bration of ghosts.
The symbolic funeral of the government.

These people from Yoga magazine who are organizing this party are going to turn the city upside-down!
We're going to go too - dressed as ghosts!
Hmm.
We'll get our own back!
And it won't be us...
...because ghosts don't exist!
HA!
Look, the city's made him mad!
Ha ha ha ha...
Is the commandant inside?
He must not be disturbed when he's with his collection.
How strange. That's exactly what I wanted to do.
Commandant, are you there?
I am. Come in and join me for a skullfull of Grand Ry...

I've studied your plan to invade Yugoslavia.
We don't have any rations.
No reserves of munitions.
We have 4,000 men, and the Slavs, 300,000.
No spare equipment.
Is there any chance you have a tiny bit of good news?
I don't know whether it's good or bad news, but the Yoga group is organizing a celebration for the dead.
Guido...
Guido is right: we'll finish on a high note. Let's go to the party!
Where are they going?
What the hell are they doing?
Click!
There's a guy following us...
I saw him!
Let's draw him towards the cemetery.

CERASI
PAOLO VITTORINI
ENZO
DONDINA! Stop!
Mr. Dondina...
Come, come, Bertoni...
Don't take your hands out of your pockets!
I have something to say to you!
Natale and Lauriano are committing a robbery!
Lauriano? He's committing nothing at all - we bumped him off this morning!
I just saw him, he's alive!
Either he's telling tales, or you screwed up again, Nerone.
It's not possible!
And why would you say that?
That's my business!

I'm going. They're hanging about the carabinieri's barracks – it's up to you to sort it out!
Make up for your bullshit! Finish him off.
Sorry, Nerone, but you made too many mistakes.
We're going to take the team and find Lauriano and Natale.
Your holsters are empty... so you had your pistols in your pockets!
You're less stupid than Bertoni and Natale, you are.

?
Excuse me...
?
Lauriano, still doing your cat routine?
You're always hiding.
I have to - the Milanese tried to kill me!
Can I sneak under your newspaper?
Ha!

Your admirers aren't very happy...
You shouldn't keep your admirers too happy, or they'll keep admiring you.
Then you and I are leaving the city.
Natale and I are doing a heist tonight.
Really?
But how?
Look at the poster on the wall there.
LA SERA
UN R
...
"The Great Celebration of Ghosts. Fantasy will destroy power, and laughter will bury it."
Nice programme...

So that's it! You've decided to bury the war?
Maybe it's better than declaring a new one.
The cortège of the protest will go all the way to the outposts, and there will be enough confusion for us to pass through.
BOO!
Ha ha ha ha ha
We're ghosts.
Ghosts are rising from the ground.
It must be time.
The children were the first to appear, eager to show off their masks...
OUUU
OOOUUUUUU
UUUUU
...followed by their parents for the parade.
The activists came out when night fell.

Families, soldiers, the bourgeois, thrill-seekers, revolutionaries and artists all flowed into the funeral cortège for "Power".
THE POWER
Everyone had something they wanted to bury from the past.
THE POWER
He's coming out, that's our cue!
Let him disappear into the crowd.
Sorry.
'Scuse us!
Coming through!

We've brought a trunk for Captain Ruffolo!
?
His luggage came yester-day...
This trunk got left behind at the port!
The captain has just gone out. We need the key from the secretary's office on the next floor.
Yup!
The guard let you in?
He fell for it.
Do you have a plan to get the statue out?
So you brought Lauriano in on the heist?
Well...
yes.
How much is your take?
Well, nothing - I'm doing it for the sake of it.
It's a Dadaist gesture. It's great.
Mmm... superb!

To make it look realistic, would you rather we tie you up or knock you out?
Err...
Tie me up.
Wouldn't it be more Dadaist to tie him up and knock him out?
Thanks for every-thing, Italo.
Lauriano, we're going to hell for that.
Pull it down a bit, his feet aren't touching the ground.
Hold on tight.
He's sliding.
?

Ruffolo, here's your mask.
That's me?
Look at yourself in the mirror.
Are you sure about what we're about to do?
They'll say it's not us!
You're using a knife?
I'm a medieval sort of man.
How are we going to find the Milanese?
Look down there, you see that wave in the crowd?

Right, left, right, left. It's Dondina.
Boss, the carabinieri!
So what? We're masked!
But Natale is the carabinieri!
Mina's waiting for us in the alley down there.
It'll take us all night to get there.
?

They were Milanese under their masks!
They shot the saint. That'll bring them bad luck.
Lauriano?!
Is there enough room for us in your rig?
Get in, quick!
We'll take the backstreets to avoid the crowd.
Masked madmen!
They shot into the crowd!

There, more bodies!
Not a pretty sight.
How awful.
We did it! We're at the outposts!
Let me push people back!
They caught us off guard...
Help us dig a grave for power!
We're honouring our dead!
Join us!
We are the ghosts of your brothers!
Lift the siege on Fiume!
Help us!
They're talking to us!
There are a lot of soldiers there, no?
Natale, open the panel at the top!

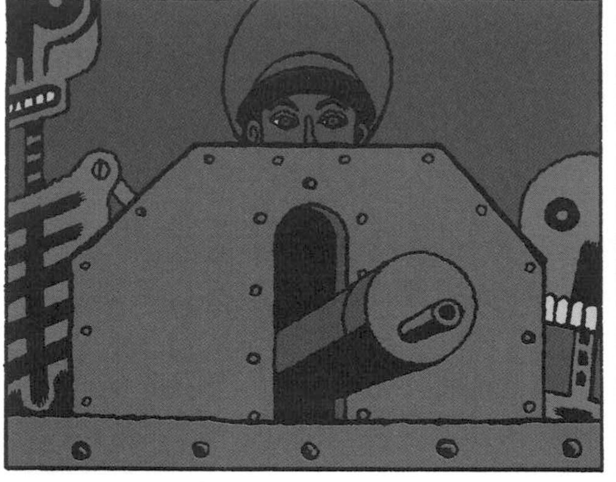

I've never seen him in real life!

Hey in there!
Hurry up and come out so this lot stops believing in miracles!
I don't think they'll stop believing in miracles or wooden saints any time soon.
Thanks all the same!
We made it! Thank you, Saint Francis!
I'm stifling in here, I'd like to get some air...
Lauriano thought, "Leone, that was your funeral, and this city is your grave. Are we quits now?"

On 12 November, the Treaty of Rappolo recognized Fiume as an independent city. The resistance had lost its ground, but D'Annunzio resisted.
On 24 December, the Italian warship Andrea Doria bombarded the government building.
The Italian army attacked on 31 December, and Guido Keller charged with a sabre and came out without a scratch, though the fighting left more than twenty dead.
D'Annunzio still wanted to believe but fatigue overcame all his supporters. He fled the city on 18 January 1921 and took refuge in Venice.

In Trieste, Natale disappeared into the shadows as soon as the statue was sold and the money shared out.
In Rome, Mina found a spot to sing in a little hall.
Then she sang in a bigger one, and then another that was bigger again, where she packed out the house every night.
Lauriano wrote articles for the *Incidents de la Nuit*, each time under a different pseudonym.
He tried to remain as invisible as possible in everything he did.
He heeded all his senses, looking out for signs of the Land of No-Where.
He didn't see Leone's ghost in a crowd any more, and he missed it.
When Mina left him, he was mildly surprised.
Do you remember the song I sang for you in Fiume?

"Then suddenly, they'll get angry at each other, and stupidly, they'll leave each other..."
"Love doesn't care about lovers!"
Well, that's now.
Oh...
But I'm not even angry...
Will you have some-thing?
I have to go.
Nn
GA"